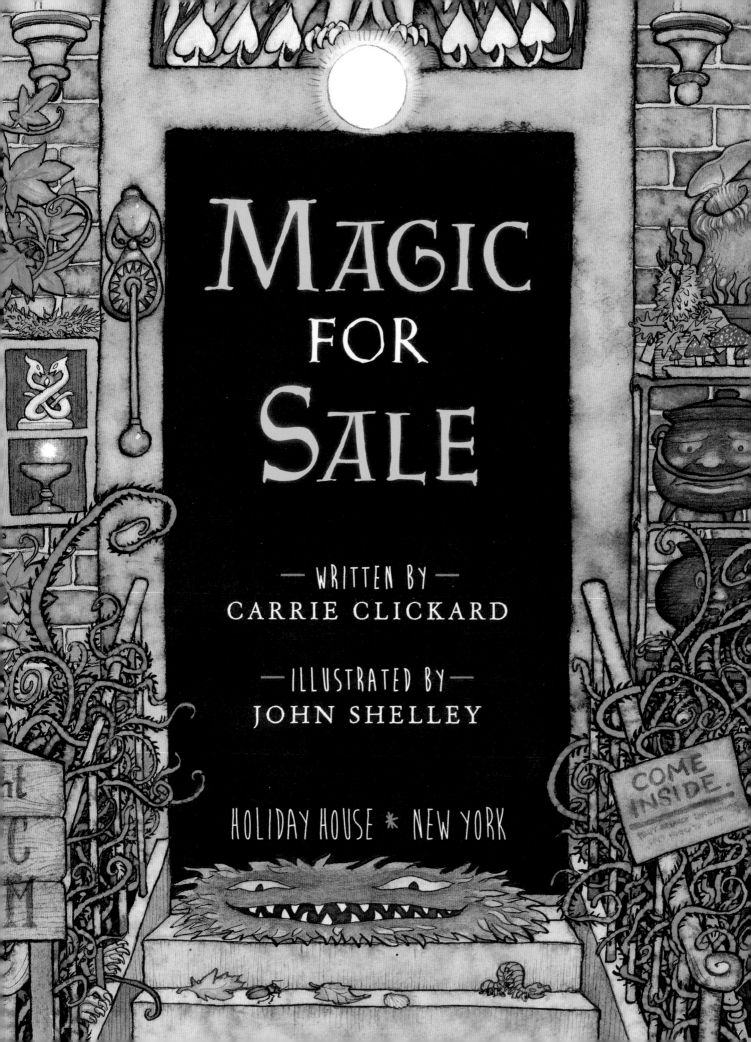

MAGIC FOR SALE

— WRITTEN BY —
CARRIE CLICKARD

— ILLUSTRATED BY —
JOHN SHELLEY

HOLIDAY HOUSE * NEW YORK

COME INSIDE.

For Sylvie who saw the possibilities
and Gumbee who haunts me still.
—C.C.

For my sister, Suzanne.
—J.S.

Text copyright © 2017 by Carrie Clickard
Illustrations copyright © 2017 by John Shelley
All Rights Reserved
HOLIDAY HOUSE is registered in
the U.S. Patent and Trademark Office.
Printed and bound in March 2017 at
Toppan Leefung, DongGuan City, China.
The artwork was created in pen and India ink with
watercolor on Canson Moulin du Roy watercolor paper.
www.holidayhouse.com
First Edition
1 3 5 7 9 10 8 6 4 2

Library of Congress Cataloging-in-Publication Data
Names: Clickard, Carrie (Carrie L.) | Shelley, John,
1959- illustrator. | Title: Magic for sale / by Carrie Clickard;
illustrations, John Shelley. | Description: First edition.
New York : Holiday House, [2016] | Summary: A young boy
tracks down an elusive ghost in the hidden rooms of a
fantastical magic shop. | Identifiers: LCCN 2015022312
ISBN 9780823435593 (hardcover)
Subjects: | CYAC: Stories in rhyme. | Magic—Fiction.
Ghosts—Fiction. | Classification: LCC PZ8.3.C563
Mag 2016 | DDC [E]—dc23 LC record available
at http://lccn.loc.gov/2015022312

ON the corner of Hemlock and Blight
skulks the shop of Miss Pustula Night,
with a sign on the stair:
"COME INSIDE. BUT BEWARE:
THE UNWELCOME MAT'S LIKELY TO BITE!"

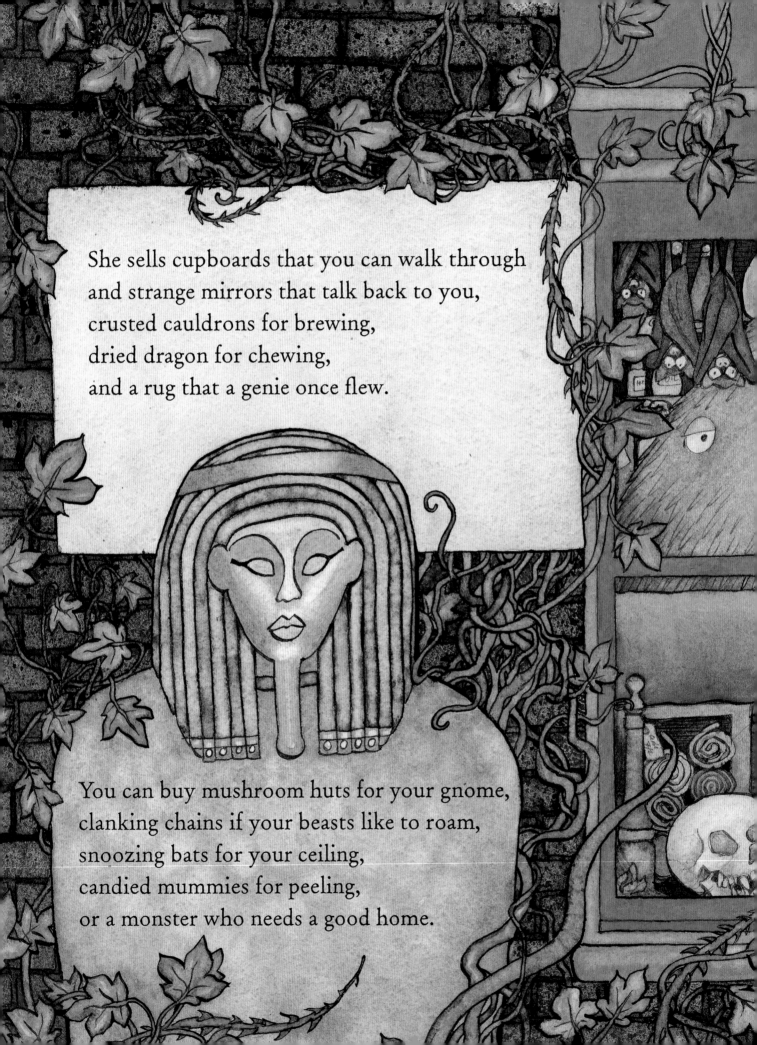

She sells cupboards that you can walk through
and strange mirrors that talk back to you,
crusted cauldrons for brewing,
dried dragon for chewing,
and a rug that a genie once flew.

You can buy mushroom huts for your gnome,
clanking chains if your beasts like to roam,
snoozing bats for your ceiling,
candied mummies for peeling,
or a monster who needs a good home.

But it wasn't these marvels and more
that lured Georgie McQuist to the store.
Miss Night kept a ghost hidden
in a room marked **FORBIDDEN**
where her customers couldn't explore.

FORBIDDEN

And though all the town's children had tried,
the shop specter had never been spied.
Georgie'd been *double* dared
so he came well prepared. . . .
He was going ghost hunting inside!

Creeaaakkk...

Georgie snuck to the store's darkest shelf
and slid next to the fresh pickled elf.

There he stayed out of sight
'til the doors were locked tight,

and he had the whole place to himself.

Then he peered past strange plants and perfumes,
pawed through caskets and baskets and brooms,
'til he tripped on a trap
and—**BANG!**—down flipped a flap,
and he dropped to the shop's hidden rooms.
"OOOF!"

"Oh, what NOW?" Georgie heard someone say.
"There's no Ghostal Delivery today!"
He lay still as a boulder
'til a hand squeezed his shoulder.

"It's ALIVE!"

"It's a GHOST!"

"Run awaaayyyyyy!"

Georgie giggled. "Wait! *You* can't be scared.
You're the reason I got double dared!"
The ghost poked out his head.
"I can't help being dead.
But scary? Not me!" he declared.

"I got caught painting stripes on the sphinx
with Miss Night's rarest vanishing inks.
When she fed it a pest
or an unwanted guest,
they would crawl right back out
through the chinks.

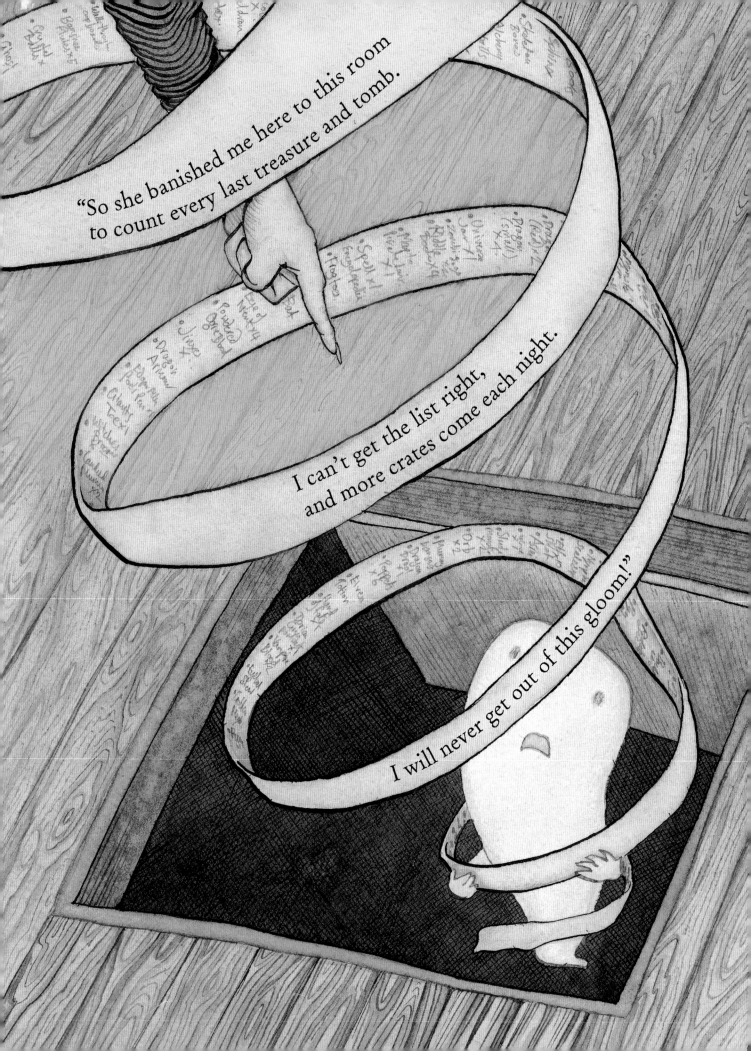

The ghost slumped on a coffin to pout.
Georgie said, "Hey, since I can't get out,
let me help with your list.
We'll be sure nothing's missed.
Now let's see, where's the minced monster snout?"

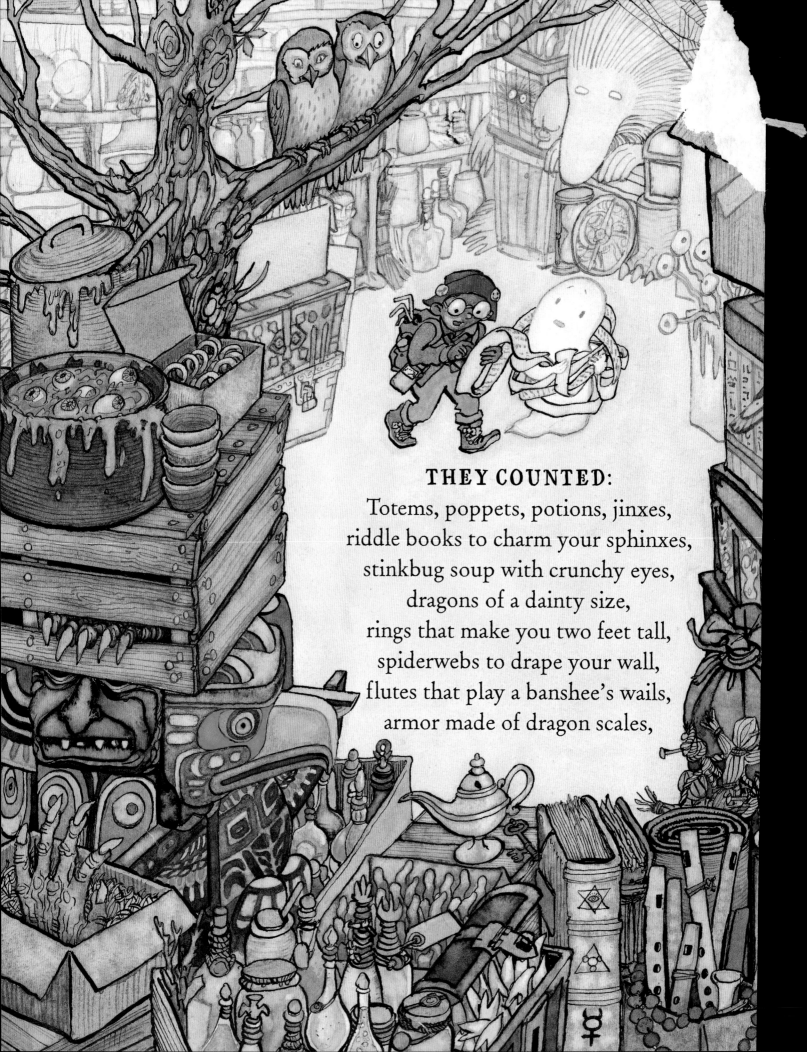

THEY COUNTED:
Totems, poppets, potions, jinxes,
riddle books to charm your sphinxes,
stinkbug soup with crunchy eyes,
dragons of a dainty size,
rings that make you two feet tall,
spiderwebs to drape your wall,
flutes that play a banshee's wails,
armor made of dragon scales,

talking owls complete with tree,
a book on ancient alchemy,
a gruesome giant's hairy toe,
the pen of Edgar Allan Poe,
a wishing toad with warty spots,
a zombie dog that
never rots . . .

Tarot cards and crystal balls,
a ghost to haunt your
castle's halls,

snakes pulled from Medusa's hair,
a map to find a pirate's lair,

freeze-dried ghoul
and dragon drool,

a kraken for your
swimming pool,

They were done—every spell, spook, and scare!
"BOO-hooray!" The ghost swirled through the air.
"Now I'd like to help YOU.
Tell me what I can do."
Georgie shrugged. "I just came for the dare."

"But I've got to get out of this store
and back home to my bedroom
before—"

Then **KA-BOOM!** came the snap
of the trapdoor's big flap,
and Miss Night landed **THUMP!** on the floor.

"I was tucked in my four-ghoster bed
quite enjoying some beetles on bread
when your ruckus and rumpus
woke Fifi and Grumpus,
so we've come down to eat *you* instead."

"Oh no, PLEASE!" The ghost twisted his sheet.
"Take a look. With his help, IT'S COMPLETE!"

Miss Night snatched up the list.
"I see three things you missed:
One young pest and two big hairy feet.

"If you're here when I've counted to four,
then young man, you'll belong to my store.
Take your monster and scat."
"He's not mine!"
"Tell *him* that. Out you go!"
And she showed them the door.

"Don't go yet!" the ghost slid out to say.
"Since I'm not stuck downstairs, we could play.
How 'bout Wednesday next week?
We can play hide-and-shriek!"
"Count me in!" Georgie said.
"Boo-hooray!"

Georgie turned to his monster and said,
"Let's get home before Mom checks my bed."
He had faced his friends' dare,
and tomorrow he'd *share*...

It was *their* turn to be scared instead!